Peachtree ST

ALL ABOARD, GEORGIA!

To Norah:
"Keep Georgia on
your mind..."
Maggie Bunn
Rosalind Bunn

WRITTEN BY
ROSALIND AND MAGGIE BUNN

ILLUSTRATED BY
KELLER PYLE

PELICAN PUBLISHING
NEW ORLEANS 2021

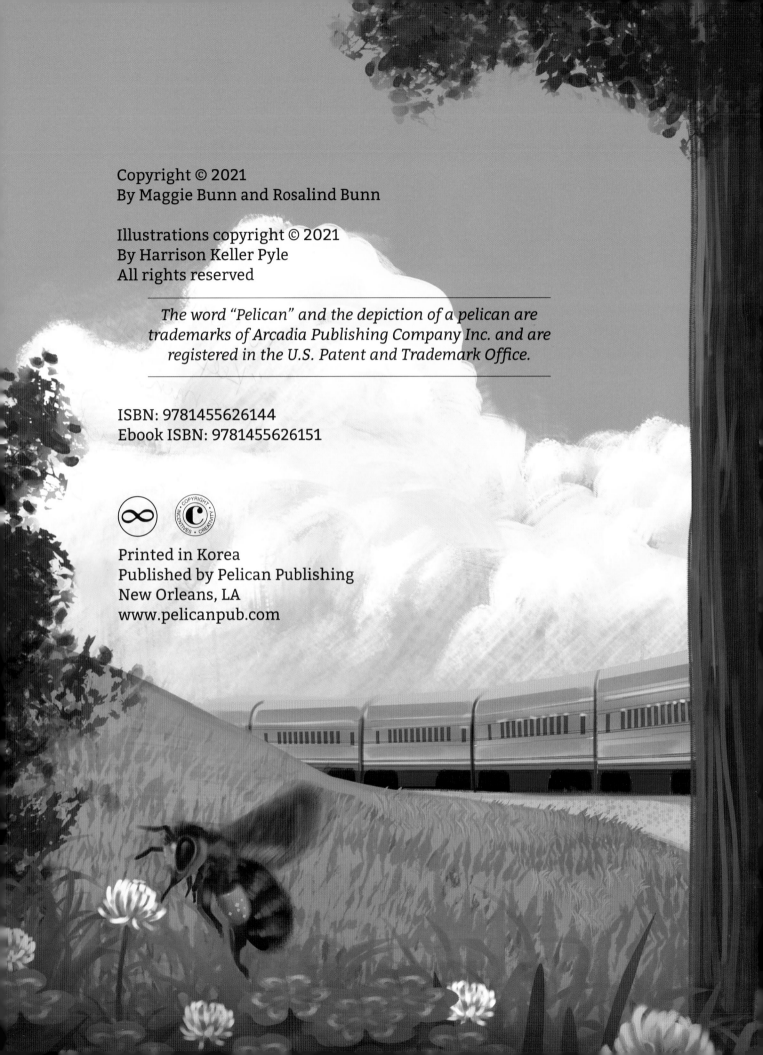

ISBN: 9781455626144
Ebook ISBN: 9781455626151

Printed in Korea
Published by Pelican Publishing
New Orleans, LA
www.pelicanpub.com

To our sweet Georgia girl, Nyla Mae
and to our friend, Shirley, who continues to encourage
this writing journey—M. B. and R. B.

To my loving mother, who taught me
everything I know—H. K. P.

I was so excited. I could not wait
to ride the train around Georgia, my home state.

I boarded the Piedmont Pacer to head to the first stop.
The Appalachian region of Georgia is up top.

Lookout Mountain was so beautiful to see.
Three states in one view—
Georgia, Alabama, and Tennessee!

We thought of a time, not so long ago, when Martin Luther King Jr.'s speech famously echoed.

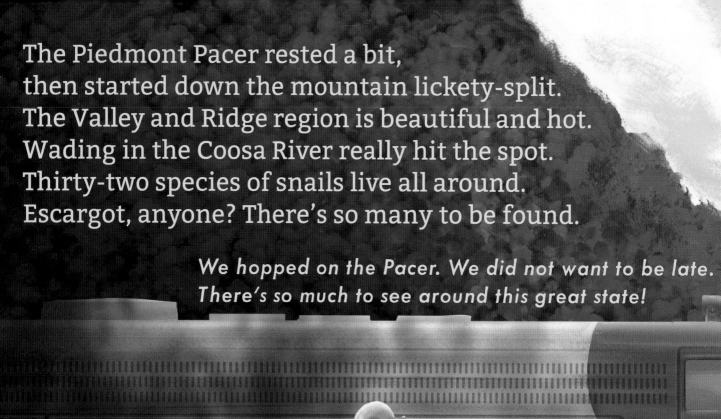

The Piedmont Pacer rested a bit,
then started down the mountain lickety-split.
The Valley and Ridge region is beautiful and hot.
Wading in the Coosa River really hit the spot.
Thirty-two species of snails live all around.
Escargot, anyone? There's so many to be found.

We hopped on the Pacer. We did not want to be late.
There's so much to see around this great state!

The Pacer chugged into Blue Ridge.
We became excited as we crossed an old gold mine bridge.
Dahlonega was the next stop on the route.
Panning for gold is the best adventure, no doubt.
I looked up above and saw Brasstown Bald.
I could imagine the early settlers' haul.

It was like going back in time
as we strolled through downtown.
The homemade ice cream
was the best treat hands down.

We hopped on the Pacer. We did not want to be late.
There's so much to see around this great state!

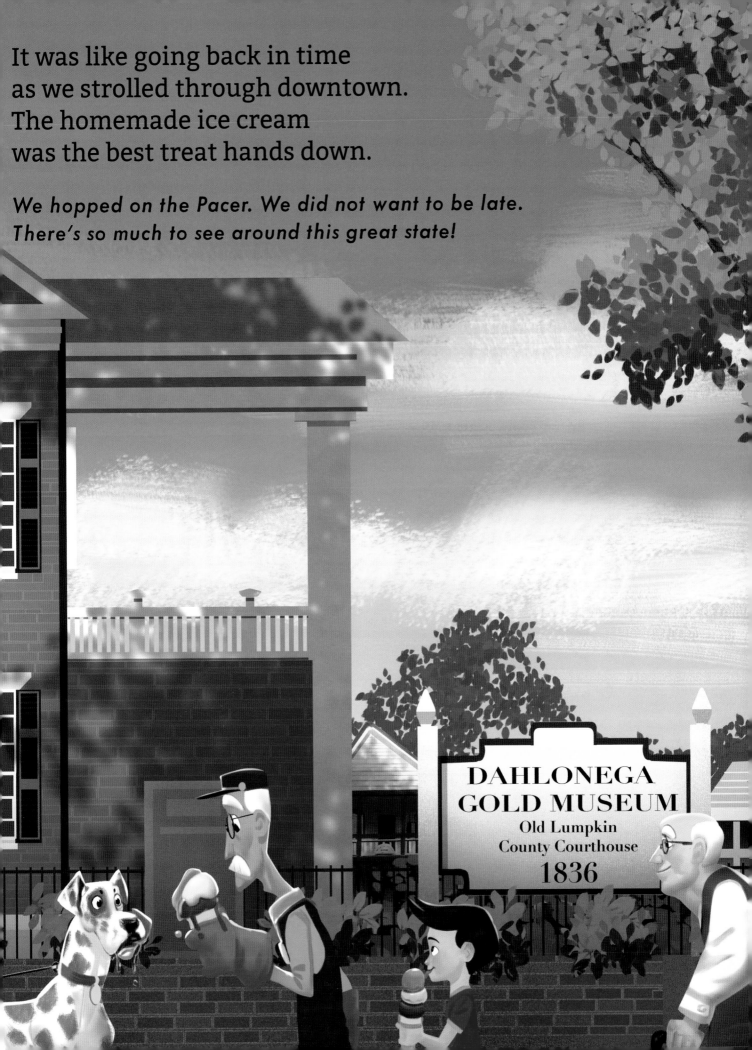

DAHLONEGA
GOLD MUSEUM
Old Lumpkin
County Courthouse
1836

The Piedmont Pacer chugged into its namesake,
the Piedmont region of my state.
We passed the Big Chicken and Kennesaw Mountain too.
On to Atlanta! Will we stop at the Zoo?

BIG CHICKEN

ATLANTA ZOO

NNESAW MOUNTIAN

We headed down Peachtree and had an ice-cold Coke.
It was refreshing. Georgia heat is no joke.
We climbed Stone Mountain and made it to the top.
We hope there is time to rest before the next stop.

We hopped on the Pacer. We did not want to be late.
There's so much to see around this great state!

The Coastal Plains was next on the list.
The Pacer slowed down so nothing would be missed.
We passed fields of peanuts and cotton.
The farmers' hard work is not forgotten.
Peach and pecan orchards dotted the land.
I could almost touch those fuzzy peaches
with my outstretched hand.

Moss in trees began to appear.
The Pacer stopped next to an old, wooden pier.
It's just like I imagined! The Okefenokee Swamp was here.
Alligators were swimming in the water below.
Be careful! Don't jump in or you might lose a toe.

We hopped on the Pacer. We did not want to be late.
There's so much to see around this great state!

On to Savannah where Tomochichi once roamed.
He was chief of the Yamacraw Indians and this land was his home.
The Squares were so beautiful with reminders of history.
The missing bench from *Forrest Gump* is still a big mystery.

SHAVER, bookseller

We feasted on Thin Mints
and rode down River Street.
There were steamboats, souvenirs,
and many tourists to meet.

We hopped on the Pacer. We did not want to be late.
There's so much to see around this great state!

The sun was setting as we saw the lighthouse.
The Pacer slowed down to let us climb out.
We felt the warm sand between our toes
and watched the waves as they fell and rose.

I grabbed my journal
as the sun set
to write about my adventures
so I wouldn't forget.
My home state is amazing
and here to explore.
With so much to see,
another trip is in store.

Choo, choo!

Authors' Note

All Aboard, Georgia was written as a picture book for young children to share all the wonderful things there are to see and experience in the state of Georgia. Maggie grew up in Georgia and learned all about the regions in third grade. As a family, we visited each one and have many fond memories. We hope you enjoy your first train ride with us.

Maggie and Rosalind

Five Regions of Georgia

Valley and Ridge

This region is in the northwest part of the state. The "ridges" are a series of limestone capped mountain ranges. They are separated by flat farming lands that were created over thousands of years of erosion. There are many waterfalls here. Iron mining is important in this region. Most of the land is covered by forests with fields of grain, pastures of cows, and orchards of apples. Many bird and butterfly watchers come visit this area.

Appalachian

This region is in the northwesternmost corner of the state. The Appalachian Trail begins here and it stretches all the way to Maine. Most of this region is covered with forest. The wood industry and furniture making are very important for this area. Other main products are corn and soybeans. It is a very mountainous region with many streams and rivers flowing through it.

Blue Ridge

Many Native American tribes hunted and fished at the foot of the Blue Ridge Mountains. Georgia's highest point, Brasstown Bald, is here at 4,784 feet. The region is known for its traditional, folk, and bluegrass music. Tobacco is the main cash crop, but corn, tomatoes, apples, and peaches also grow here. This region contains the starting points of both the Chattahoochee and Savannah rivers. There are many trails and campgrounds around for tourists to enjoy.

Piedmont

This region takes up 30 percent of the state, stretching from Alabama to South Carolina. Atlanta, the state's capitol, is in this region. This is the place that many tourists visit. It also has the highest population of all the regions. Piedmont is a combination of the two Italian words: "pied" (foot) and "mont" (hills), which means that the area is at the "foot" or bottom of a mountain range. This region is known for their pecans, peanuts, and peaches.

Coastal Plain

This region is the largest in the state. Peanuts and Vidalia onions are major crops here. It is divided into the upper and lower coastal plain. The upper region is the farming/agricultural area and the lower contains the Okeefenokee Swamp. This swamp is the largest body of freshwater in the state. Part of the Atlantic Ocean touches the Plain.

But when the angry bear saw how polite Papa was, he remembered his manners too. He explained that he had stopped short because a mama duck and her ducklings had crossed in front of him. Then he and Papa Bear looked at their bumpers and saw that no harm had been done.

"As I was saying," said Papa as they continued on their way, "it's very important for us to remember our manners at all times—and I want to thank you, Sister, for reminding me to remember mine."

"You're very welcome, I'm sure," said Sister Bear politely.